Micky Monkey
gets lost

Story by Sue Barnett

Text by Sue Barnett
Ingrid van den Berg

Published by
HPH Publishing

Micky the Vervet monkey was with his mother and the rest of his monkey troop, swinging through the trees looking for food, when it all happened.

They were far from Maduma Boma where they lived.

A big thunderstorm came up.

The sky turned darker and darker. Streaks of lightning split the sky. Thunder rumbled all around.

'What's happening?' Micky cried.

This was his first thunderstorm and he was scared. He held on to his mother and hid his face in her fur.

Big drops of rain began to fall onto the leaves. Micky could smell the rain and feel the cold raindrops on his face. Soon the rain was pouring down in torrents.

Suddenly, there was a loud thunder-clap so close by that in fright Micky lost his grip on his mother. He fell all the way to the ground.

'Mommy! Mommy!' he called. But the thunder was so loud that his mother didn't hear him. All the monkeys took fright and sped away through the treetops, leaving Micky behind.

He was alone. The troop was gone. His mother was gone.

'What am I going to do?' whimpered Micky. He was feeling very cold and lonely.

Micky was too young to know about the dangerous animals in the area.

There were snakes.

There were baboons.

Then there were lions.

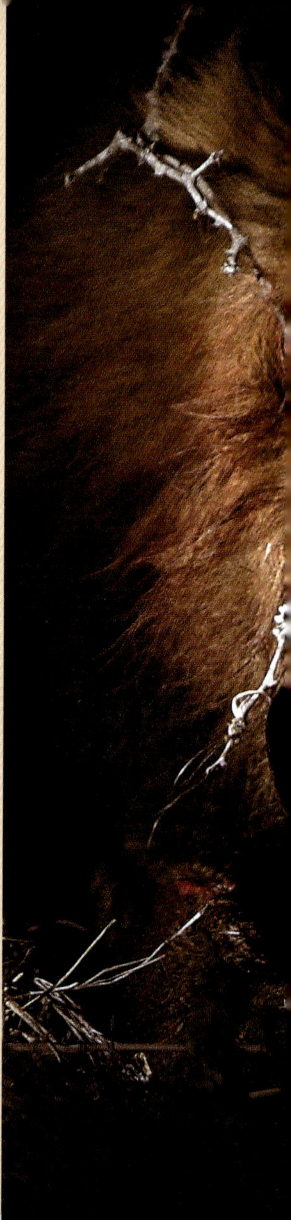

And hyenas.

And caracals.

Micky knew it wasn't safe to be on his own.

The most dangerous were the leopards. Micky's mother had warned him about them. They can see and hunt in the dark.

The rain stopped. The night was coming.

'I had better find a safe place to sleep,' Micky said.

He found a hole in a hollow tree trunk and crept into it.

Micky curled up into a little ball, making himself as small as possible to keep warm. He listened, hoping he would hear his mother, but he heard only strange night sounds which frightened him. He put his hands over his ears.

'I must be brave. I am sure Mom will find me in the morning,' he said to himself. He was so tired that he soon fell fast asleep.

When Micky woke early the next morning, he was shivering from the cold. He climbed back into the tree and watched the sun rising. The sun soon warmed him and he felt much better.

'I'd better just wait here for Mom to find me. I'm sure she will be coming soon.'

He waited and waited. Then he climbed all the way to the top of the tree and looked over the bush-veld as far as he could see. He saw impalas and warthogs, but he could not see his mother.

'Mommy! Mommy!' he called, then listened – all he heard were zebras barking in the distance.

He called again and listened – still no answer.

Micky knew his mother would not abandon him. He said to himself, 'I must just be brave and wait for her.'

The sun rose higher and higher and it became hotter and hotter. Micky dozed off in the sun. He woke with a start. Something was nibbling his toe.

It was a squirrel. He watched the nimble little animal racing up and down the tree and it made him laugh. He was happy to have the squirrel's company. He didn't feel so alone.

Later a giraffe came to eat from the tree. Micky was fascinated by the giraffe's long tongue. 'Don't the thorns hurt your tongue?' he asked the giraffe.

The giraffe just smiled at him and carried on eating. He was friendly and pulled funny faces. This also made Micky laugh.

While waiting in the tree, Micky smelt something strange. He didn't know the smell, but the hair on the back of his neck stood up when he looked down. It was a lioness.

The lioness sniffed around the tree and looked straight up to where Micky was hiding.

She tried climbing the tree but kept falling down. It was a very tall tree and lions are not the best tree climbers. After a while she gave up and left.

Micky breathed a sigh of relief.

He became tired and fell asleep again. He dreamed of his mother and all his friends at Maduma Boma.

Suddenly, he was awakened. Something was shaking his tree and shaking it so hard that seedpods were breaking off and falling to the ground below.

One seedpod fell right on his head. Micky's eyes grew wide with surprise and he clung on tightly.

An elephant was leaning against the tree trunk to push it over. 'Oh no, please don't do that!' Micky shouted.

The elephant looked up. 'Sorry, little monkey, I didn't see you up there,' he said in a deep voice.

'Have you seen any monkeys around here today?' asked Micky.

'No I am sorry, I haven't seen any,' replied the elephant.

This made Micky sad. He was tired, scared, thirsty and lost.

'Perhaps I should be brave and go and look for my mother,' Micky said to himself.

He climbed down the tree.

While hopping through the long grass, Micky heard a hissing sound.

He was inquisitive and went to investigate. It was a snake but Micky didn't know that. It struck at him and he jumped up in the air in fright.

He decided that he didn't like the look of this long, scaly creature and scampered away before it could bite him.

Micky climbed into some bushes where he felt safer. A movement in the sky overhead caught his eye and a shadow passed over him. His heart almost stopped. What was that? Was it an eagle? Micky hid and kept really still. After a while, the eagle flew away.

Just when he thought that his troubles were over, he heard loud snoring coming from above him. He looked up and saw a leopard fast asleep on a branch high above his head.

'That must be a leopard. I had better not wake him up,' he whispered.

He slowly crept down the tree and quietly climbed through the bushes. When he found an open plain, he started running.

He ran and ran as fast as he could. As he ran, he looked back to see if the leopard was following him. Because he wasn't looking where he was going, he ran straight into a big, smelly hyena.

'Ahaa ahaa ahaaaa. Look what we have here,' laughed the hyena. 'A tasty little snack.'

The hyena's breath smelled awful. Micky was pinned beneath him and could not escape. It was slobbering all over him and laughing hysterically. Micky was terrified. Then suddenly the laughing stopped.

The hyena looked up, straight over Micky's head and then bolted.

Micky was relieved, but he was afraid of looking to see what had scared the hyena off.

It was a man!

The man picked him up and said, 'Oh you poor little monkey. Where's your family? Have you lost your mother?'

The man's name was Barry and he lifted Micky up and gave him a cuddle.

Barry said, 'We'll find my wife and see if she can find you something to drink.' He took Micky back to his home.

Barry's wife Sue managed to find a baby's bottle and some milk. Micky was so thirsty that he drank every

drop. The milk tasted just like his mother's milk.

Afterwards, he closed his eyes and fell fast asleep. He slept for a long time. When he woke up, he felt much better.

'Where am I?' he wondered for a moment, but he soon realized that he was in a sarong around Sue's waist. She was carrying him around just like his mother did and he felt safe.

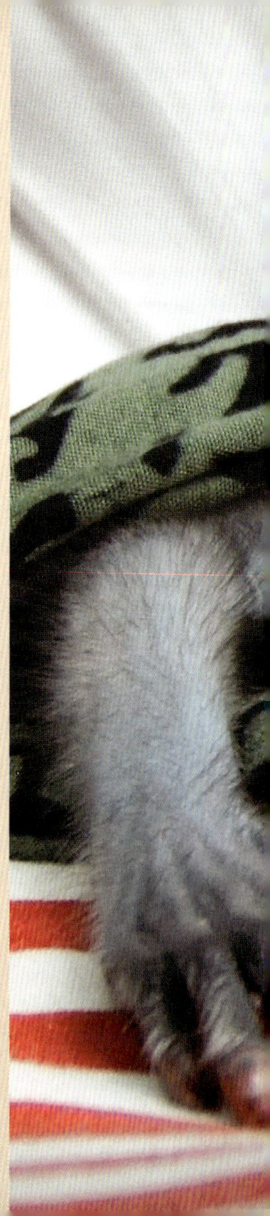

Sue took Micky to visit her mother and sister and they gave him lots of cuddles. He enjoyed the cuddles but this made him miss his mother and monkey family even more.

'The people are kind, but where, oh where is my mother?' he asked.

Sue drove all over the farm, looking high and low in all the trees and bushes for Micky's mother.

The troop of monkeys were nowhere to be seen.

The sun was beginning to set. 'Please, please, let us find my mother,' Micky thought to himself. He was really worried. He didn't want to be alone in the dark for another night. He didn't want to be cold and scared

again. He didn't want to run away from lions or hissing snakes or eagles or snoring leopards or smelly hyenas anymore. But he also didn't want to stay with these people forever. He just wanted to go home.

After a while, Sue and Micky reached a big tree. Sue put Micky on the ground and walked away.

Micky started crying. 'No, no, please don't leave me alone!' It was getting dark and there were so many dangerous animals about.

He cried even louder.

'Doesn't anybody want me?' he cried.

All of a sudden, monkeys' heads popped out from the treetops all around him. It was his troop of monkeys. They had heard him crying and Sue had known that they were there – that was why she had left him behind.

Micky's mother jumped from the tree, snatched him up and hugged and hugged him. They were both so happy to see each other again.

'Where were you? I've been looking everywhere for you,' whispered his mother into his ear.

Micky immediately stopped crying. He was so relieved to be in his mother's arms again. While she quickly fed him, the whole troop gathered round to welcome him home.

Then with a warning to him to hang on tightly under her stomach, she leaped back into the tree and climbed up to a safe spot to settle down for the night.

'I missed you Mommy,' Micky said.

Micky had had a very bad experience. He now knew that he needed to stay close to his mother for protection. He knew that his mother loved him dearly.

He also knew that he must always hold on tightly to his mother no matter how frightened he gets. He had been a very lucky monkey to be rescued and have had help in finding his mother again.

In the years that followed, Micky grew up and became a brave, strong monkey. He learnt monkey ways while playing with his friends. Later he became the leader of his own troop and lived happily on Maduma Boma.

THE END

Vervet monkey facts

Vervet monkeys occur only in Africa.

They favour big trees close to water and are quite common in the bushveld.

Vervet monkeys live in troops of up to 20 individuals. Adult males and females, as well as young ones of varying ages, make up the troop. Members of the troop stay together for the sake of safety. They spend the nights in their favourite sleeping tree, snuggling close together for warmth.

Monkey babies are born with a pink face and blackish fur. After three months, the fur gradually turns grey and the face black.

At about three years of age, they are proper monkey teenagers. It takes four to five years for a male to reach maturity. Vervet monkeys can reach an age of about 12 years.

Vervet monkeys feed on fruits, plants, insects and smaller animals. They also go for birds' eggs. They find their food on the ground or in trees.

Monkeys are intelligent and may become problem animals when they get too used to humans. People should not feed them since this encourages them to raid houses for food. They can become aggressive when they cannot get what they want and then they use their big canines to defend themselves.

When they sense or see danger, they utter warning sounds. They make many different sounds, each one has its own meaning.

Monkeys like to groom each other. They remove tiny bits of skin and parasites such as ticks and fleas from each other's fur. These make nice monkey tit-bits which go straight into the mouth.

Young monkeys love to play – it makes them agile and deft.

The tail of the vervet monkey is longer than its body. Measured from the tip of the snout to the tip of the tail, monkeys may measure a metre or longer.

A large adult male can weigh up to eight kilograms.

ISBN: 978-0-620-61079-7
Published by **HPH Publishing**
PO Box 13244
Cascades, 3202
E-mail: info@hphpublishing.co.za
Website: www.hphpublishing.co.za
Tel: +27 86 171 0327
First published in 2014

Text by Susan Barnett and Ingrid van den Berg
Photography by Heinrich van den Berg, Philip van den Berg, Susan Barnett, Chris Coetzee and Jan Sebesta
Edited by John Deane and Gillian Paizes
Proofread by Gillian Paizes
Design, typesetting and reproduction by Heinrich van den Berg
Printed and bound in TWP Sdn. Bhd., Malaysia